Pirate Power Play!

Pirate Power Play!

Helaine Becker

Illustrated by
Sampar

Scholastic Canada Ltd.
Toronto New York London Auckland Sydney
Mexico City New Delhi Hong Kong Buenos Aires

Scholastic Canada Ltd.
604 King Street West, Toronto, Ontario M5V 1E1, Canada

Scholastic Inc.
557 Broadway, New York, NY 10012, USA

Scholastic Australia Pty Limited
PO Box 579, Gosford, NSW 2250, Australia

Scholastic New Zealand Limited
Private Bag 94407, Greenmount, Auckland, New Zealand

Scholastic Ltd.
Euston House, 24 Eversholt Street, London NW1 1OB, UK

Library and Archives Canada Cataloguing in Publication
Becker, Helaine, 1961-

Pirate power play / Helaine Becker ; illustrated by Sampar.
(Looney Bay All-Stars)

ISBN 0-439-94619-0

I. Sampar II. Title. III. Series.
PS8553.E295532P57 2006   jC813'.6   C2006-902255-0

6 5 4 3 2 1   Printed in Canada   06 07 08 09 10

Contents

Chapter 1

None of this story would have ever happened if Reese McSkittles hadn't left his right mitten behind at the rink.

It had been a great hockey practice — maybe the best practice the Looney Bay All-Stars had ever had. Randall Wetherbury had suddenly mastered skating backward, so that he no longer kept smashing bum-first into the boards. The Teeny Weeny Heany Twins

were awesome "Pillars of Power" on the defensive line. And Shannon Weiss's slapshot sizzled in a way it never had before.

Reese was so thrilled by the change that he was halfway home before he realized one of his mittens was missing. He knew that if he was late for dinner again, his mother would shred him into lobster salad. But what if he returned home without the mitten, so lovingly knitted by Grandma Buckminster?

He turned back.

It was nearly dark by the time Reese got to the rink. He hunted everywhere for the mitten. It was not on the bench. It was not under the bench. Reese got down on his hands and knees to search behind the bench. He found a Three

Musketeers wrapper and a grotty old coin, but no mitten.

He flicked away the wrapper, dumped the coin in his pocket and kept searching. Just as Reese's thumb touched

a nasty blob of frozen chewing gum, he felt a big, hairy hand grip the back of his neck.

Suddenly Reese was yanked to his feet. The pirate — for the big, hairy hand did belong to a pirate — put his face right up to Reese's.

"What have we here?" boomed the pirate's big, hairy voice. "A wee land-lubber, methinks!"

"Let me go, you creep!" Reese shouted. He kicked the pirate in the knee, bit him on the wrist, pinched him in the armpit, but still couldn't break free.

"Yo, ho, ho!" laughed the pirate. He lifted Reese off the ground with one meaty fist. "You are a bonny and spirited lad," he nodded approvingly. "I think I'll keep you. Look what I found, me boys!

A new navvy to do our chores!"

Shapes began to gather in the shadows. There were four, eight, then twenty pirates! "Hooray! Hooray!" rose the cheers from the pirate crew. "Someone else to swab the deck!"

The captain — for the pirate gripping Reese was indeed the captain — shook Reese. "Our ship, the *Mistress of*

Doom, lies yonder in that dark cove. You come quietly, lad, or we'll feed you to the fish."

"Okay!" Reese squirmed. "Just put me down!"

The pirate dropped him with a thunk. "Now step lively, or we'll carry you by your toes!"

"Aye, aye, I guess," Reese muttered.

He shouldered his hockey bag, fell into line behind the captain and reluctantly marched into the darkness.

Chapter 2

The pirates snaked along a narrow path to the cove. A ghostly ship loomed out of the mist. Reese gazed up in awe at the ship's Jolly Roger. "I didn't know there were still pirates. Not for real, I mean."

"No pirates?" gasped the captain. "Why, that's like saying there's no stars and no water! You must be daft, lad. There have been pirates in these parts

for two hundred years and more!

"Why, my granddaddy on my mum's side called Looney Bay home, and he was none other than Blackbeard himself. And my granddaddy on my dad's side was that ruthless scourge of the sea, Bluebeard. He had a cottage

here. Liked to come for a pillage each summer.

"When the old ones died, my mum and dad took over the family business, see? Then I came along. I was named for my granddads: Captain Black-and-Bluebeard. That's me!"

"I've heard of you, but I always thought those were just stories," said Reese.

"Stories!" roared Black-and-Bluebeard.

"How can they be just stories with what you have written on your shirt? Don't it say Looney Bay? Why, Looney Bay's meant buccaneering and swashbuckling since before the time of dinosaurs! How can you be saying there be no such thing as pirates, when you're practically a pirate yourself?"

"Actually, sir," stammered Reese, "I'm a right wing."

The pirates all stopped. They looked at Reese strangely.

"Right wing," Reese said. "Like on a hockey team? The Looney Bay All-Stars is a hockey team."

The pirates just kept staring at Reese.

"Don't tell me you don't know what hockey is." Now it was Reese's turn to stare.

"I can't believe you guys haven't heard of hockey," he muttered, shaking his head in disgust. "You might be pirates," he sniffed, "but you sure aren't *Canadians*."

"Why, you little puppy!" growled Black-and-Bluebeard, grabbing Reese by the throat. "I'll teach you to watch your words with the greatest pirate that ever lived! We'll throw him in the brig, boys!"

The next thing Reese knew, he was in a stinking cell, deep inside the pirate

ship. On the other side of his barred window he could see the pirates. They were swinging in hammocks, singing sea shanties off key and playing Go Fish.

As Reese's eyes adjusted to the gloom, he saw that the hold was jam-packed with ill-gotten booty. Tall piles of stolen goods threatened to topple onto the pirates from all sides. Some of the stacks twinkled with gold and jewels, but not all of them. Most were made up of treasure of an entirely different sort.

There were piles of woolly tuques.

There were chests filled to bursting with scarves and knee socks.

There were scads of watches and mood rings and winter boots, pencils and notebooks and soggy lunches.

There were dolls galore, some missing hair, some missing arms — all of them missing their owners.

There were stuffed animals, baseball gloves and soccer balls, running shoes

and umbrellas and flip-flops, sunscreen and sun hats, ski pants and underpants.

There, in the bowels of the *Mistress of Doom,* were all the items that had ever been lost by the kids of Looney Bay. They had not been lost at all — they'd been stolen by the pirates!

On the top of an overflowing trunk, Reese spied a familiar object. It was a striped mitten. The very same mitten so lovingly knitted by Grandma Buckminster — for him!

Why those dastardly, cowardly thieves, fumed Reese. *I'll show them! I'll stop them! But how?* He was helpless as long as he was stuck in the brig. He needed a plan.

Chapter
3

Reese leaned his forehead against the cold, rusty bars. He stuffed his hands in his pockets and was surprised to find the old coin he had picked up at the arena. He rolled it back and forth between his  thumb and forefinger to help him think.

He thought and he thought.

Then he had an idea.

It was a very good idea.

He waited until one of the pirates said to another, "Have you got any threes?"

Then Reese started chuckling softly to himself — but still loudly enough for the pirates to hear.

"What are you laughing at?" snarled the one-eyed pirate.

"Nothing," said Reese. Then he chuckled again.

"You find us funny, do you? Remember it's you who's in the brig."

"Well if I were out there with you, I certainly

wouldn't be playing Go Fish," snorted Reese. "That's a game for babies."

"Why you dirty, rotten, no-good…"

"Tough guys, like us All-Stars," said Reese, "leave card games to the land-lubbers. We play hockey. Now that's a proper pirate game."

"Oh yeah? How do you play then?" asked One-Eyed Elmer.

"You'll have to let me out to show you."

The pirates whispered together for a moment. Then the one with a scar shaped like a hot dog bun said, "All right. We'll let you out. We're kind of tired of this game ourselves. But no funny business — or the captain will feed you to the fish!"

Reese heard the jangling of keys, and then the door to his cell swung open with a loud creak. He was out of the brig!

"First, we need a puck. And two nets for goals..." Reese began.

Under Reese's direction, the pirates converted the deck into a rink. They

flooded it with water. By morning it had frozen solid. Then they strung two hammocks between pairs of pikes for the goals. Barrel staves became sticks. An old bung from a barrel made a pretty fair puck. Rusty sabres were fitted to leather thongs and tied to boots for skates. The pirates wobbled on their

blades at first, but their sea legs helped
them keep their balance.

Every evening, after a hard day of
looting, the pirates would
unwind by learning
about hockey. They
would practice their wrist
shots against the bulwarks

and perform endless passing drills. They were naturals at bodychecking and were pretty good at fast breaks, too.

The pirates caught on quickly. Before long, they had played their first half-decent pick-up game (The Looters beat the Pillagers 20–12). Even Captain Black-and-Bluebeard played now and again.

It wasn't the NHL, but it was hockey. Sort of.

Finally, Reese's moment came.

Over a cold supper of maggoty rice and squid, the pirates were rehashing some of the week's greatest plays:

"Remember when Shorty deked around Macdubbins and scored on

He shoots, he scores!

Cutlass Carl? That was sweet."

"That was nothing compared to the play I made around the post," bragged One-Eyed Elmer.

"You mean all that shameful slashing and spearing you did?" snarled Toby Mory. "That wasn't fair hockey, and you know it!"

"Yo, ho, ho!" Elmer replied. "Fair's what you want? From a pirate? It's in me blood to be stealing the puck, and anything else I can from you! Slashing is only fitting for a fine fellow like me! You're lucky I didn't toss you over the boards!"

Bandyleg Bert nodded and chuckled. "Ah, quit your whining, Toby. That's the way hockey's meant to be played."

Reese gave a delicate sniff.

"What?" asked Elmer.

"What, what?" said Reese innocently.

"You sniffed."

"I did?"

"Yes, you did. Like you had something to say."

"Me? Nooo…" said Reese, his voice trailing off — as if he did indeed have something to say.

Black-and-Bluebeard grabbed Reese by the shirt front and hoisted him so his legs dangled in the air. "Out with it," he demanded.

"What do you want me to say? You guys are pretty good. For *beginners*."

A cry rang up from the pirates. "For *beginners?* Why, you…"

"And you think there are better players than us, do you, lad?" accused the captain. "Are you insulting our honour?"

"Nooo…of course not, Captain. It's just that, well, compared to the Looney Bay All-Stars—"

"Your old sandbox playmates, you mean?" The captain's eyes narrowed, and he pulled Reese close to his face. Reese counted four oat flakes, one lima bean and a bird's egg — just hatched — in the thicket of the blue-black beard. "Are you saying you don't think these fine lads could give a showing to a bunch of babies in nappies?"

The crew roared with laughter. *"Baby, baby, stick your head in gravy!"* they chanted.

Reese looked Captain Black-and-Bluebeard right in the eye. "I think the Looney Bay All-Stars would swab the deck with you. Easy-peasy."

"Are you challenging me and my boys to a good old hockey game?" the captain asked.

"Aye, I think I am," replied Reese.

The captain stroked his beard. "So it's a wager then. What do we get from you if we win?" he asked.

"You'll have to parley with the captain of the All-Stars for your answer," Reese said. "I can go on your behalf."

"Aye, it's the way it's done," nodded Black-and-Bluebeard. He snapped his head toward his men. "Elmer, Cutlass Carl, go with him. And watch that he doesn't pull a fast one or…"

"We know," said Elmer and Carl together. "You'll be feeding us to the fish."

Chapter 4

It was the end of the second period and the All-Stars were down 2–1 to the Trinity Bay Marauders. As Captain Laura Hook drank deeply from the water fountain, she heard the clank of chains at her elbow.

"It's me," whispered Reese.

"Reese!" Laura exclaimed. "Where have you been? We've been worried sick about you! Your mum—"

"Not now," said Reese. "I'm in trouble and I need your help. You, and the rest of the team." He quickly explained. He could see Cutlass Carl's sword glinting at the edge of his vision.

When he finished the story, Laura whistled under her breath. "I'll talk to the rest of the gang. We'll have your answer by the end of the third period."

Reese shuffled his feet nervously as he waited for the game to end. He knew Elmer and Carl were watching the game too, sizing up the opposition. Were the All-Stars really up to the challenge? Reese sure hoped so, but he was scared. The All-Stars were good hockey players, but they were just kids. Black-and-Bluebeard and his crew were — *gulp!* — pirates. Grown-up pirates!

With one minute to go in the third period, Shannon Weiss scored for the All-Stars with a slapshot to the upper right corner. The game was tied. At the buzzer, Laura came skating over to Reese at breakneck speed. She swished to a stop just in front of Cutlass Carl. The blades of her skates sprayed him with ice.

Laura unsnapped her helmet and wiped the sweat off her brow.

When she spoke, her voice was grim. "Reese, I never told you this before, but I've got some history with your pirate pals. My great-great-great-great granddaddy, Ephesius Mortimer Hoop, was the captain of a survey ship in His Majesty's Royal Navy.

"One day, while he was doing a survey of these very waters, Hoop's sloop was raided by pirates. The pirates showed no mercy. It was a bloody fight. My granddaddy was able to beat them off, but he lost twelve of his best men and his own right hand in the battle. That's when he changed his name from Hoop to Hook.

"Ephesius vowed revenge on the devil

who dared attack one of the King's ships, but he never got it. He died without meeting his sworn enemy again. That enemy," Laura grimaced, "was Pictou Pete, the father of your captor.

"So you'd better believe I'm with you, Reese, and so are the rest of the All-Stars. You tell those pirates we'll face them tomorrow on the ice. If we win, you go free and the *Mistress of Doom* is forfeit to us. If we lose — which we won't — they'll have a new bunch of navvies to swab their dastardly decks! And you can tell Captain Black-and-Bluebeard that his *real* Mistress of Doom waits ashore. And her name" — Laura pulled herself up to her full height — "is Captain Laura Jane Ephesius Hook.

"Now I've got a game to win, Reese. Good luck!" Laura said as she headed back to centre ice for the overtime tiebreaker.

"Laura?" Reese called out.

"Yeah?" she replied, looking back over her shoulder.

"We're gonna make your Great-Grandpa Hook proud."

* * *

Back on board the *Mistress of Doom*, Black-and-Bluebeard turned to the crew. "What do you say, boys? Shall we accept the terms of the parley?"

"Accept! Accept!" shouted the pirates.

"I accept your offer," the captain told Reese, bowing with a flourish. "I'll send Cutlass Carl back to your captain with a dispatch stating the time and date. That's official pirate style." He sat down at his desk to pen the note. "What was your captain's name again, boy?"

"Laura. Laura Hook."

"Captain Hook! The very same? Why you dirty scoundrel! You never said!"

"You never asked," smirked Reese.

The captain pushed back his chair and kicked it out of his way. He paced the floor, rubbing his hands together. "So this is how it shall be. I will face my enemy at last — not from behind a cannon, but from behind the red line!"

Chapter 5

The next morning, the pirate crew rowed to shore in the *Mistress of Doom*'s dinghies. One-Eyed Elmer held a fist up to Reese's face. "Don't think we'll give ye up without a fight, deck-swabber," he sneered. "We've gotten fond of you."

Reese did not reply. He still said nothing as the dinghy scraped the stony beach. It wasn't until they reached the

All-Stars' shabby old rink that he spoke. "May the best team win," he said with great dignity. He held out his hand. His wrists were chafed where his chains had bitten into them.

Captain Black-and-Bluebeard nodded. He solemnly shook Reese's hand. "Aye, that we will." The pirate's grin was dark and cold.

* * *

Reese got to the home team locker room and found the All-Stars suited up and ready to go. Laura tossed a set of pads to him and helped him with his jersey. "Glad you're home safe," she said.

"Home, but not safe," he replied. "It's do or die." He flexed his fingers in his gloves.

"No worries. You can count on us. We'll teach those pirates not to mess with our right wing!" said the Teeny Weeny Heany Twins, placing their own gloved hands on Reese's.

"Can do!" chimed in the rest of the team. They added their hands to the stack.

"Will do," said Captain Hook as she rose to her feet. Her forehead was creased with determination. "Let's go!"

* * *

The ice was fast, and the All-Stars had the early advantage. They dominated the play with their expert skating and superior teamwork. The pirates, however, made up for their lack of skill with sheer nastiness. Five minutes into the game they had broken every rule in the book. Twice.

By the end of the first period, three penalties had been called against the pirates for slashing. There would have been more, but Captain Black-and-Bluebeard had pitched the ref over the boards into the stands.

The pirate goalie, Cutlass Carl, put a

plank across his net. He told the All-Stars he'd defend it to the death.

Shorty, who'd already been kicked out of the game, tossed a grappling hook over the scoreboard and swung himself across the rink. He dropped into the All-Stars' crease and smacked his stick on the ice to let his teammates

know he was open. No one dared to call
him offside.

At the same time, the pirates had
pinned Darren to his goalposts with his
stick and drew a large X on his chest.

Then, with a bloodcurdling shriek,
the pirates charged!

The All-Stars nimbly fended them off,

but were called for high-sticking.

The score remained 0–0 at the end of the first period.

"We are not playing like a team!" Captain Hook berated the exhausted All-Stars. "Where is that passing? Keep the puck moving, fast, fast, fast! We have the home-ice advantage! We can't let Black-and-Bluebeard beat us! Do you want to spend the rest of your lives swabbing the deck of his ship?"

On the other side of the rink, Black-and-Bluebeard threatened the pirates. "It is your honour and the *Mistress of Doom* at stake! Win this game or you'll be fish food, every last one of you!"

Halfway through the second period, Teeny Weeny Bryan Heany snagged the puck from One-Eyed Elmer and shovelled it over to Hook. Hook passed it to Weiss on the blue line. Weiss swivelled her shoulders and slapped the puck hard. It whistled into the net — the All-Stars had scored!

The pirates came back in the third period, hard and fast. They took shot

after shot on net, but Darren Willett stopped every one.

With the clock winding down, it looked like the All-Stars were about to put away a victory.

Then, with three minutes left, Cutlass Carl slashed Ryan Heany, knocking him to his knees. Carl bunny-hopped over him — it was a buccaneer breakaway! Darren did his best, but was no match for the pirate and his parrot.

Cutlass Carl fired off a sizzler. The pirates scored!

"This is it, guys," urged Laura as the teams faced off at centre ice. "Give it your all! Go Looney Bay!"

"Go Looneys, go!" the All-Stars shouted back.

Darren cupped his hand to his mouth to make the team cheer: the haunting cry of the Ring-Necked Loon.

The puck dropped.

The All-Stars won the face-off. Weiss to Hook, Hook to McSkittles, McSkittles back to Weiss. Weiss was closing in on the net...

"Not on yer life, me bonny lass!"
Captain Black-and-Bluebeard hollered.

Then, with a terrible cry of "Yo, ho, ho!" he hooked Weiss from behind. She was caught — the puck was loose!

But along came McSkittles, whooshing out from behind the net. He found the puck.

As the clock wound down, Reese cocked his wrists for a last desperate shot. He swiped at the puck. It was going…going…*Ping!* No! Had it hit the crossbar?

Everyone held their breath.

Then they watched as the puck dropped like a stone… inside the net.

The All-Stars had won the game!

At the buzzer, Reese cheered, "I'm free! I'm free!" He skated back to celebrate with his teammates.

"You won't be stealing any more treasure or kids from Looney Bay!" crowed Ryan.

"Oh, yeah?" snarled One-Eyed Elmer. "You think you're going to stop our pirating? Never! In fact, I think I'll get my new pirate season off to a roaring start by taking you hostage, stripling."

Elmer grabbed Ryan. Buccaneer Bob cheered and made a move toward Bryan.

"Forget it, barnacle breath!" shouted Reese. He zoomed across the ice and in one swift motion, pushed the net over onto Buccaneer Bob. At the far end of the rink, Darren Willett did the same to Cutlass Carl.

Bloodcurdling pirate yells filled the
air. Swords were drawn. Sticks were
raised. Would the All-Stars have to com-
pete again, this time against the pirates'
deadly swords?

They stood steady, but then, above
the din, Captain Black-and-Bluebeard's
voice rang out. "Leave off, me maties!
The jig is up, and the battle lost. They
won their freedom, and our booty, fair
and square!"

He dropped his stick.

He flung down his sword.

He threw his hat down, too. As his crew and the All-Stars watched in awe, Captain Black-and-Bluebeard sat on the ice, legs splayed, and started to weep. "Vanquished by a pack of wee brats," he wailed. "I'm over! I'm done! I'm a failure at the pirate game!"

"Actually, you were a darn good pirate. You're just a lousy hockey player," said Laura Hook, placing her hand on his shoulder. "Too bad for you the *Mistress of Doom* and all that treasure is ours."

"Woe is me! What will we do? I'm nothing without me fine lady! I cannot leave me ship!"

Reese skated over. "I've got an idea," he said, with a mischievous grin…

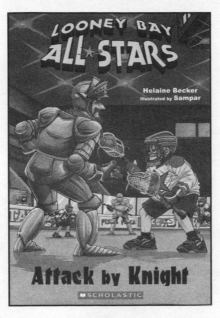

Coming Soon!
Looney Bay All-Stars
Attack By Knight

Reese's class trip to the museum is so boring.
But when he runs into two real-life knights who
started a duel hundreds of years ago,
things get way more interesting.
Not wanting the knights to hurt each other, Reese
comes up with a plan. And with the help of the
rest of the Looney Bay All-Stars, the two knights
decide to settle their differences in a more
modern way — on the lacrosse court!